The Snot Gang in 'Gotcha!'

Mary Gallagher

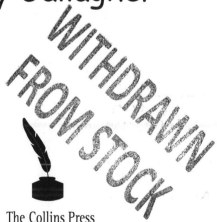

The Collins Press

Published in 2005 by
The Collins Press
West Link Park
Doughcloyne
Wilton
Cork

A Cataloguing-In-Publication data record for this book is available from the
British library

ISBN: 1-903464-71-4

Typesetting: The Collins Press

Font: Comic Sans MS, 14 point

Cover design: Deirdre O'Neill

Printed in Ireland by Colour Books Ltd

A School Project

I don't think I'll ever want to become an adult. OK, some adults can act normal but most of them freak me out. Take my Dad, for example. He says the silliest things like, 'If you fall off that bike and break your two legs, don't come running to me'.

My Mum isn't much better. 'Are you back?' she asked me the other day when I came home from school early. I mean, there I was standing right in front of her!

My Aunt Marjorie has an image problem. There is more hair on her chin than on

1

my Dad's head. My dad says that Uncle Harry could well do with some of Aunt Marjorie's chin hair to cover his bald patch. It's so embarrassing when I call around for my cousin Joe. She always insists on giving me a big wet smacker.

Then there's Uncle Harry. He spends his day pottering around the garden talking to the plants. My Dad says it's because he wants to escape from my Aunt Marjorie who keeps nagging him to go jogging. Uncle Harry is round and podgy and had to retire early from work due to a 'funny' heart. When Miss Coll, producer of our school pantomime, was one dwarf short I asked Mum if I could suggest my Uncle Harry. She gave me one of those dangerous looks that adults give you sometimes that freezes you to the spot. So what? I was only trying to help. I thought it might give Uncle Harry a break away from all the nagging. That's the thing about adults. Sometimes they are hard to figure out.

Talking of Miss Coll and teachers – they

have got to be the saddest lot on the planet. I won't go into that, except to tell you how I got myself roped in to do a stupid school project last year by the weirdest of weirdos – our history teacher, Mr Roog. He has definitely got to top the list of saddest adults ever. He arrives every day, armed with huge volumes of history books. He, is bald, apart from two pieces of electrified hair which stand out on each side of his head like antennae to pick up signals from God knows where. These signals definitely don't come from the world that you or I live in. No! Mr Roog lives in a world where normal people like you and I wouldn't dare to go. He took some sort of mad craze that the students in his class should do a local history project during the Halloween break. Of course, it never occurred to him that the word 'break' should mean free time. 'The devil makes work for idle hands' is his favourite saying. He gave us one week to come up with an idea.

When he asked us for our ideas that

Friday, my friend Max said, 'Sir! I racked my brains all week but I can't think of a thing'.

'Roogie' answered in his posh voice, 'Rack it again you silly boy!'

My cousin Joe was next. 'I was thinking I might try to prove the existence of UFOs,' stammered Joe. Everyone giggled and Joe went red. Of course, it never occurred to Joe that history was about the past and UFOs were very much a new thing.

'UFOs!' shouted Roogie. 'What has that got to do with local history? Anyway, the whole world has been trying to prove the existence of UFOs for years. What makes you think that a tiny pea brain like yours can suddenly come up with an answer?'

Poor Joe looked like he was going to cry. I started to laugh and Mr Roog saw me.

'And as for you ... you Miss Shaw, what little gem have you got in mind?' he asked. I gulped.

'I thought I might do a study of ... lep-rechauns.' There. It was out. They were

old, weren't they? There was silence. Only the ticking of the clock could be heard. I felt like a right nerd. How could I say such a stupid thing? Then Roogie's face lit up and broke into one of his rare smiles. A gold tooth winked down at me.

'You mean from a local and social viewpoint?'

What the heck was the old bat on about now? I thought it better to say 'yes' even though I hadn't a clue what the old codger was saying.

'Yes, Mr Roog, I mean exactly that.'

5

I looked over at Max and Joe in triumph. They were looking at me dumbstruck, as were the rest of the class. All these years there had been a genius in their class and they hadn't recognised her!

'You understand, Holly, that it would have to be all your own work! I couldn't give you any help.'

'I understand perfectly, Mr Roog.'

'You might be onto something here Holly,' he wittered on, excitedly.

MAX, JOE AND HOLLY

Max is short for Maxwell Arnold Cooper. He is not the 'brightest star in the sky', as far as school is concerned. However, Max is always game for a laugh. He lives with his Mum and Dad and big sister Helen not too far from my house. Helen is training to become a beautician and lives most of the time on cloud nine. She tries to model herself on the soap stars. She is presently working part time in the local theatre as a make-up artist.

Joe Deen is my cousin. Joe is a bit of a

dreamer but like Max he is good fun to be with. Joe lives with my Aunt Marjorie, Uncle Harry and big brother Ben, who comes home at weekends from boarding school in Dublin.

Me? I am just an ordinary kid trying to live my life in an ordinary way. This means that I try to avoid as much adult contact as I can. Don't get me wrong – I love my Mum and Dad. It's when a whole lot of adults get together that I try to make myself scarce.

I also think that my Mum and Dad could have picked better names for my four-year-old twin brothers, Sylvester and Stanley. I mean, let's face it – Sylvester Shaw and Stanley Shaw? I go red with embarrassment every time I think of it.

It's because of those names that I had trouble bonding with them at the beginning. My Dad says it was pure jealousy, as I had the run of the place until they came along.

Anyway, I love them to bits now and I owe them big time for the way they keep the relations off my back. It's their turn now to get prodded and poked. You know when adults line you up to see who each one looks like?

'Why! Holly is the image of you dear', my Aunt Amy used to say to her husband – my Uncle Frank. Oh, thanks a bunch, I used to think, looking at the great 'orang-utan' beside her. Do you know that there's more hair coming down my Uncle

Frank's nose than on a chimney-sweeper's brush? It does wonders for your self-esteem! At family gatherings my gran would poke me in the ribs and say, 'She's very pale dear. Are you sure she isn't ... ?' And she would whisper the rest in my Mum's ear while the others would look at me as if I was an exhibit at the zoo. Then I would panic.

'What is she saying? What's wrong with me?' I'd ask.

'Gran was just wondering if you were constipated dear!' Mum would reply, Then, I would go all red – and no wonder! Discussing someone else's toilet affairs in front of the whole world! At least now Sylvester and Stanley are the centre of attention and I can escape the very minute I hear of a family get together.

Now for the really, really embarrassing bit! Joe, Max and I go back a long way, in fact way back to 'The Snotty Tots Playschool' in Lisnashee. It was my Dad who started it.

'How is the Snot Gang today?' he would ask every day, as he came to pick us up. Then he would laugh, as if it was a great joke. The thing is, the name stuck but not without a reason. In those days Max was a disgusting little sod – even more disgusting than he is today. His nose was always dripping snots and he never seemed to have a hanky.

'Yuck!' I used to say. 'You are disgusting!'

'So what! They are my snots!' Max would argue.

After a few years we finally gave up and now we don't even notice. That is why we are still called the 'Snot Gang' to this day!

Looking for Help

Anyway, to get back to the project – 'What was that all about?' asked Max, as we headed home after history class that Friday evening.

'Some Halloween break this is going to be, and why did you have to pick me?' he asked.

'Yeah! You might have asked us first,' said Joe.

'Count yourselves lucky I picked you,' I replied. 'Otherwise Mr Roog would have made you do one of your own. This way we can work as a team.'

I haven't gone around with Max and Joe this long without knowing how to hoodwink them into my way of thinking. I felt they would fall for it!

'That's alright,' I continued. 'I'll go and tell Roogie that you'd prefer to do your own project.'

'But you can't do that,' wailed Max. 'I don't have any idea for a project.'

'I don't either,' said Joe.

'Well lads, it looks like you are both stuck with me and let's face it, at least this way you won't have to come up with any more ideas. Didn't Ben get an A in history last term?' I asked.

'I think so,' replied Joe. 'Why do you ask?'

'Well, with his help, this should be easy,' I replied.

I know Ben loves history and all that geeky stuff. He would know enough about leprechauns to keep Mr Roog off our backs. I was going to suggest that Helen,

13

Max's sister, might help us too but I suddenly remembered the last essay she wrote for me, where every second spelling was wrong and I thought better of it. I couldn't face two more days in detention. Secretly I was thinking I could off load the information that Ben would give us on to Max and Joe and they could write it all down. If I played my cards right I could plan the whole project so I would get all the credit.

'I think you should both go for it!' I said, thinking they would never fall for my suggestion. To my surprise, two big smiles lit up their faces. If some bright spark ever decides to re-make the film 'Dumb and Dumber', Max and Joe would be perfect for the main parts.

'Ok, you can count us in,' they said together.

One of the reasons Joe, Max and I always got on is that we don't worry about anything, particularly not schoolwork. We had it all planned in our heads. Ben could do our research through the Internet. Who knows? He might even type it up for us as well. We would do a bit of artwork ourselves. That should please old 'Roogie'! No, there was nothing to worry about! Roll on the Halloween break! We had it all sorted!

However, Ben was having none of it. Ben is at that strange stage of life where he is bordering between teen and adult. He is always up in his room playing some awful din on his guitar.

The three of us knocked on Ben's bedroom door and went in.

'What do you three spacers want?' he glowered. His hair was long and oily. He was wearing little round specs that weren't much bigger than his eyes.

'We have a project to do Ben,' said Joe sweetly. 'We wondered could you ...'

'Out! Now! All three of you!' roared Ben, pushing us onto the landing and shutting the door behind us.

'What now?' asked Max.

'We have to use some other tactic,' I

15

suggested, not feeling too hopeful.

'We only have a few weeks until we have to hand it in,' whined Joe. 'What are we going to do?'

For the first time in our lives, Joe, Max and I were beginning to worry just a little bit.

'We will have to go it alone,' I sighed.

However, after half an hour, we had given up. We didn't even know where to begin. This was an emergency. We were now so desperate we decided to ask Helen. Max's parents were out when we arrived and Helen answered the door in her bathrobe. Her face was caked in dark brown mud.

'Oh, it's the Snot Gang!' she said, as she let us in. 'Thank God it's no one important!'

Another boost to the self-esteem! Why do people not appreciate us kids, especially other family members? Parents always want their kids to be like someone else's. 'Look at Billy Jones. How come he likes piano lessons? His parents must be really proud of him' or 'I bet that nice Linda

Larkin doesn't give guff to her parents', or 'Why can't you walk up straight like that nice Brady boy?' They might as well just stick a poster on our backs that reads, 'This is my freak of a daughter/son. Be thankful she/he isn't yours!' Maybe Billy Jones' parents point me out to him and say, 'Look at that nice girl Holly Shaw ... She's always so pleasant looking', or 'That Holly Shaw looks like a really nice girl'.

When I asked my Dad if he thought this could be he muttered something like 'silly git' and walked off muttering to himself.

Anyway, we were now at Helen's mercy. We followed her into the kitchen where every beauty product under the sun was spread across the table.

'We were wondering if you could help us with our school project?' I asked her politely.

'What is the project about?' she asked.

'Leprechauns and fairies', replied Max. Helen went into hoots of laughter.

'Leprechauns and fairies?' she roared. 'Surely you don't believe that crap.'

I could see we were off to a good start. When she saw Joe's worried face, she softened.

'Well folks! It isn't really my type of thing but I suppose I could try,' she said doubtfully. 'Now, you will have to wait until I take off this mudpack and put on my face.' She disappeared into the bathroom.

'What does she mean "put on her

face"?' whispered Joe.

'Oh! She means that she has to put on loads of lipstick and eyeshadow and stuff,' Max explained. 'Did you know that our Helen plucks out most of her eyebrows and then draws them back on?'

How Helen and Max were related was anyone's guess. Helen was always doing herself up. Max, on the other hand, was an untidy, snotty little menace!

'What! All that pain for nothing?' I asked.

This was the person we were relying on to do an in-depth study of the little folk and life in Ireland long ago?

Holly has a Plan

As we sat in the kitchen waiting for Helen, a text message came through on her phone.

'Let's have a look,' said Max as he grabbed the phone.

'How wud u like to go to da cinema tonite? Ben', was the message.

'That must be your Ben,' I said to Joe. 'You never said that he fancied Helen.'

'First I knew of it,' said Joe and he shrugged his shoulders. 'Anyway, we shouldn't look at other people's messages.

20

It's not nice'.

Just then, Helen returned looking like a painted doll. Joe and I could see exactly what Max meant. Along her eyes were two painted-on eyebrows.

'You look nice,' I said, thinking a small lie wouldn't hurt.

'By the way, there's a message for you,' said Max, handing her the phone. Helen looked.

'Oh! It's that Ben Deane. He keeps pestering me to go out with him and I don't even like him ... Ooops! Sorry Joe. I forgot that he's your brother.'

'That's alright!' said Joe. 'I don't like him either.'

A wild idea was beginning to form in my head. It was perfect! What if we could get Helen to go on a date with Ben in return for doing our project?

'Do you mind Helen if we use your sitting room for a quick meeting before we start?' I asked. 'We have something important to discuss.'

Helen raised her newly-painted eyes.

'Alright, but don't be long.'

Max and Joe were all in favour of the idea. All we had to do was convince Helen. Did I mention Helen wasn't too bright? When we told her she asked, 'Aren't you forgetting something? I don't even like Ben Deane.'

'Aw! Come on sis!' begged Max. 'Mr Roog will skin us alive.' This was Max's big mistake.

'Oh! Will he now? If I were to agree, how much is this deal worth to you?'

A strange smile hovered around her mouth. I didn't like it one bit. Before she was finished we had promised to clean the whole house for her before her parents got back as she had promised to do it. Then we had to mow the lawn, tidy the tool shed and sweep the leaves on the path. We also had to promise to come around every Saturday for a month to do whatever chores she wanted done! In return, she promised she would go out with Ben, plead with him to help us with her project and she wouldn't dump him until he had all the work done. We had to sign our names at the bottom of a written agreement. Should we fail to turn up any Saturday, Helen would tell Ben that we tricked him and there would be hell to pay – and I thought Helen was dumb!

True to her word Helen kept her side of the bargain. Two days later, Ben came looking for us in Joe's room.

'Did you lot need help with a project?' he asked. 'I'm free this evening. I might be able to help.'

'I see now why our Helen has a mad crush on you,' lied Max, as he wiped yet another snot from his nose. 'She is forever going on about you.'

'Is she really?' asked Ben eagerly.

'Oh yeah! She is always saying how much she fancies you.' Ben beamed from ear to ear.

'Silly goofball,' I could hear Joe muttering under his breath.

'Well lads! Show me all the stuff you have gathered so far to see can I put some order on it,' Ben said.

'But that's the point. We haven't got any stuff' said Joe. 'We haven't got a clue what to do. We thought you might show us.'

'Wait a minute,' said Ben. 'You three losers want me to help you to do a project on leprechauns and you still haven't gathered any information?'

'We thought you might know better than us,' I said sweetly. 'You see, everyone talks of how brainy you are.' It didn't work.

'Look here', he said. 'Even someone with as little brains as you should know that you need local knowledge to do a local history project. Now, you can either go and enquire of older people in the area or you can go back to Mr Roog and tell him you can't do the project.'

The thought of going back to Mr Roog to tell him we had been a little too hasty soon helped to make up our minds.

'Can't you find out for us?' pleaded Joe.

'Do I look green to you lot?' Ben asked.

I was going to say that he did look

slightly different but I thought I had better not. 'If you lot think that I am going around this town asking everyone I meet about their last sighting of a leprechaun, then you can forget it. By the way, if you happen to meet one bring him around and introduce him.' Then he burst out laughing.

Fools laugh at their own jokes, my granny always says, but I thought it better not to mention that right now.

'Holly, Holly! Come and look,' shouted the twins as I arrived home. Our garden was full of squawking, squealing five-year-olds. I had forgotten it was the twins' fifth birthday. I was led over to the corner where there was a new kennel and looking out was the most frightened-looking dog I have seen in my life. The poor animal looked traumatised, and no wonder! About twenty noisy children were looking in at him. I knelt down and patted him on the head.

'Nice dog, isn't it?' I heard from behind,

and there stood my Dad dressed as an Indian.

'We got it from Mrs Smyth over the road. She says she is too old to look after it. And Mum and Dad says you have to help us to look after it,' Sylvester explained.

'Yeah, you have to help us to keep the garden and kennel clean,' added Stanley.

'Did anyone think to ask if I wanted this mutt?' I asked, but I felt sorry immediately. After all, it wasn't the poor dog's fault that he had been landed with two owners like Stanley and Sylvester.

'What is his name?' I asked, deciding to show an interest.

'Ruff' squawked a bunch of five year olds in reply.

'Nice name,' I said, as I left the garden and went indoors, leaving Ruff to the mercy of his captors.

Uncle Frank and Aunt Amy

There was nothing for it except to go around the town and try to get some information.

'My Aunt Amy works part time at the library so she might be able to help us,' I suggested, although I wasn't too keen on the idea.

'Your Uncle Frank works with old trees, doesn't he?' enquired Max. 'Maybe he might know of a place in the woods where fairies used to live?'

Joe looked over at me in despair.

'Yes Max,' said Joe wearily 'that's a brilliant idea.'

I laughed even though I didn't feel much like laughing inside.

'Uncle Frank is a wood sculptor,' I said. 'He sculpts pieces from bog oak. He digs up old oak stumps from bogs and makes all sorts of things.'

'He might make us a sculpture of a leprechaun,' said Joe. 'It would look good with our project.'

'I very much doubt it,' I replied.

We collected Ruff on the way and found Uncle Frank outside the house, frantically trying to sweep up the leaves.

'Look at this place,' he moaned. 'This lawn was like a new pin last night and now it is covered with leaves again.'

'Could you not wait until all the leaves have finished falling and then do one big sweep?' suggested Max helpfully.

'No! He couldn't', I felt like answering. Uncle Frank cannot deal with mess of any kind.

'You had better come in,' he said, not too enthusiastically. 'He will have to wait here,' continued Uncle Frank, pointing at

Ruff. I knew there would be no point in arguing, so I tied Ruff's lead to a tree.

'Tie him good and tight,' said Uncle Frank. 'I don't want him walking all over my shrubs.'

Aunt Amy's welcome wasn't much better. As soon as we walked into the polished hallway she was out with her little frilly apron tied around her.

'Now children, take care and walk on the mats. We don't want mud all over my nice clean hallway now, do we?'

I wanted to say 'There's nothing I'd like better' but instead I found myself smiling and saying, 'Of course not, Aunt Amy'.

'I bet I know why you are all here! You're trick or treating, aren't you?' she asked, and before any of us could answer she said, 'You run along with your Uncle Frank into the sitting room and I'll get us some goodies!'

I thought it was better to say nothing. Up until that moment Joe, Max and I had almost forgotten about Halloween because our minds were so taken up with the project. This was indeed Halloween. There would be a party at our house later in the evening.

Just then, Aunt Amy arrived in with a tray. I forgot to mention that she and my Uncle Frank are health food fanatics. On the tray were three glasses of Aunt Amy's favourite carrot juice, homemade wheat biscuits and a bowl of cheese cubes. 'Now children, tuck in,' said Aunt Amy enthusiastically, as Uncle Frank was arranging the cushions in a neat pile. Max and Joe's faces fell when they saw the

food but they lifted the glasses reluctantly and began to sip.

'Aunt Amy,' I began, 'are there any books on fairies or leprechauns in the library?'

'I could have a look dear,' replied Aunt Amy.

Then we explained how Mr Roog had given us this project and how little we knew.

'I have been working with bog oak for the last twenty years and I haven't seen a leprechaun yet,' laughed Uncle Frank. 'There might be the odd witch or two out tonight though.' Both he and Aunt Amy hooted laughing.

After a long struggle, we managed to get the carrot juice down. Just as well Aunt Amy and Uncle Frank don't have any children of their own, I thought, as Joe and Max chattered on. I had spent a fortnight with them a few years before when Mum went into the hospital to have the twins. When Dad had come to collect me he burst out laughing, and no wonder. I was dressed up like a trussed chicken in a pink frilly dress with matching pink frilly socks. 'She's always wearing jeans,' complained Aunt Amy 'and as for those two rough boys she goes around with? Why can't she make friends with that nice Priscilla O'Dea or Caroline O'Connor?' She and Uncle Frank had even put a barring order on Sylvester and Stanley after they accidentally broke a valuable ornament on the mantelpiece! No! Uncle Frank and Aunt Amy certainly didn't suit having kids around, or animals for that matter. Poor Ruff was glad to see us come out of the house again. Then I saw the huge hole he had dug in Uncle Frank's front lawn in his desperation to get free.

'Get that brute out of here!' shouted Uncle Frank, and poor Ruff looked terrified.

'Sorry about that,' I muttered, and was glad when we got up the road and out of sight of the house.

A Perfect End To A Busy Day

'What now?' asked Joe. 'We still have no information.'

'I think I'm going to be sick,' wailed Max. 'That juice was horrible.'

We could see the police station up ahead.

'We could ask in there,' suggested Joe. 'The police might know of somebody in the town who could help us.'

'It's worth a try,' I agreed.

In we went and Max went up to the counter.

'We need information on leprechauns,' he began, but I could see the mistake was already made.

'Did you hear that Tom?' asked the policeman whose mouth widened into a smirk. 'A young lad here looking for a lep-rechaun!'

Tom came over.

'So far we haven't seen any,' he said smiling, 'but we'll put up a poster: *Wanted Dead or Alive! A Leprechaun!* Then the two men doubled up and roared laughing.

'Wait until I tell this to the lads on patrol', spluttered the one who was not Tom.

'Starsky and Hutch think they are very smart,' said Joe as we left.

'They don't look like brain surgeons to me,' replied Max, as if he would know!

Just outside the station we saw the Rector.

'Hello children!' he greeted cheerfully. 'My! You do look glum. Whatever is the matter? It can't be that bad.'

We told him our sad story and about

35

our search for information.

'You say you have someone looking up information for you. So stop worrying. That will be enough, I'm quite sure. Here! Take this money and go and buy some sweets.' He gave us a handful of change. Then he went off whistling down the street.

'What a nice man,' I thought. Why can't all adults be like him?

Our next visit was over to Mrs Muldoon's sweet shop. When we told her our problem she took a deep breath and began to chatter.

'Let's see now. Leprechauns – little busy fellows, dressed all in green they were, little beards on them, if I remember rightly. Ah, yes! Little buckles on their shoes, lived out in the woods ...'

We were glad when the shop doorbell tinkled and another customer came in.

There was great excitement when I arrived home. Mum was baking apple tarts for the Halloween party. The twins were fitted out in their wizard costumes and

Dad was carrying in the groceries.

'I'll help you,' I offered.

Just then some bangers went off further down the street. Poor Ruff was terrified.

'Alright! He can stay indoors just for tonight,' said Mum.

Halloween in our house is very much a family affair. Grandad and Granny came over and also Uncle Harold, Aunt Marjorie, Uncle Frank and Aunt Amy. Then Dad, Grandad and the two uncles take the twins over to the bonfire on the town square and the ladies sit in and natter. Tonight would be no different, and it wasn't.

Max, Joe and I went along to the bonfire at around ten o'clock. I thought it was better to leave Ruff at home. As we approached the bonfire, Stanley and Sylvester came running over in their costumes. Max, Joe and I pretended to be frightened and they chased us around the square with squeals of delight. All the while the sky was one huge kaleidoscope of colour. It was truly magical. Thoughts of

leprechauns and fairies disappeared. We could see Helen and Ben at the far side of the square holding hands. Ben waved to us.

'I don't believe it,' said Joe. 'You would almost think he was normal. Helen is having a good effect on him.'

Later we sat on the grass and ate our toffee apples that the ladies' committee had passed around.

'Do you know?' I said to Max, 'this isn't a bad little place to grow up.'

'Agreed,' said Max.

38

We trudged home at midnight tired after our day's adventure. Granny and Grandad decided to stay over for the night. As we sipped steaming mugs of cocoa in the sittingroom before going to bed I asked them if they knew anything about leprechauns.

'You need to go to see old Mr Williams,' replied Grandad. 'He knows a lot about ancient folklore and should be able to help you.'

At last I was getting some information.

'Where does he live?' I asked.

'He lives out the Ardsberg Road,' replied Granny. 'I can draw a map for you and you should have no trouble finding him,' said Grandad. I was in a much happier frame of mind going to bed that night. I texted Joe and Max with the news and told them to meet me the following morning outside the school. As I drifted off to sleep I left the Halloween ghouls and witches to ramble on their own through the dark streets of Lisnashee.

Mr Williams

It wasn't exactly our ideal way of spending the Halloween break but next morning Max, Joe and I crossed the town and headed out the Ardsbeg Road. Ardsbeg is on the coast road and on that morning, as we walked along, we could smell and almost taste the bracing sea air that blew in from the Atlantic. About one mile from town the road forked to the left. I had a rough map that my grandad had drawn out for me. I could see from the map that Mr Williams' house was beside an old graveyard. After following the road for a bit, it sloped to the right and Max shouted, 'There it is!'

Sure enough, in the distance we could see a field with old ivy-covered head-stones. Just beyond the graveyard was one of the cutest thatched cottages I have ever seen.

'That must be it,' shouted Joe.

I knocked on the door. We could hear foot-steps. The door was opened by Mr Williams, an elderly, wise-looking man. We introduced our-selves and told him our business.

'You had better come in,' he said kindly, and we followed him into a warm, cosy kitchen. 'You must be frozen,' he said. 'I have the very thing to warm you all up.'

'You have to be careful when you are dealing with the fairy world,' said Mr Williams, as we sat around his shiny black stove drinking mugs of hot chocolate.

Right away I knew we were going to get on all right with Mr Williams. Here was a man at last who seemed to understand children!

'Then you really believe in leprechauns?' asked Max with rounded eyes.

'Well, I do and I don't,' said Mr Williams. 'Certainly, I have seen and heard some strange things in my time but I have never actually seen a leprechaun. Mind you, I know many people in the past who claimed to have seen them.'

'Gosh!' exclaimed Max. 'I would give anything to see one.' Sometimes Max does act strangely and this was one of those times. I just hate it when he puts one of these silly looks on his face. Mr Williams caught me rolling my eyes over at Joe.

'Your friend may not be as silly as you think,' said Mr Williams, laughing. 'In fact, I could bring you to a spot where a leprechaun was reported to have been seen. It is beside a well where locals always claimed it was dangerous to go and visit.'

'What do you mean dangerous?' asked Joe beginning to get as interested as Max.

'Well,' said Mr Williams, 'over the years people were supposed to have seen things at it. It was said that lights could be seen around the well at night and if the water in the well turned red as you looked in, then unlucky things were going to happen to you. Strange sightings of the "wee folk" were reported. Over the years people got afraid and no one ever visited it. In fact, not many people know it is there, it is so overgrown.'

While Mr Williams was talking, I was writing. It never occurred to Max or Joe to write anything down. Their contribution was to sit spellbound, listening to the stories with their mouths wide open.

Over the next two hours we would learn a lot about fairies and leprechauns. We learned of 'gentle places' where fairies were supposed to hang out. These were called fairy forts and were all over the place. Mr Williams explained that our own town of 'Lisnashee' meant the fort of the fairies and 'Dunshee Pass', just outside the town meant the same. The word 'Shee' means fairy and a pass was a road used by the fairies when travelling from fort to fort. If anyone built a house or shed on one of these passes, bad luck would follow.

Mr Williams then told the story of an American who built a house between two forts on top of a pass. At the housewarming party, all the plates and cups moved around the house and the roof fell in. People fell and tripped in their rush to get out. In the morning, the house disappeared and the owner returned to America.

At this stage I looked over at Joe and Max. Max's face was lit up with the excitement of it all and Joe looked flabbergasted. Of course, as usual, I kept my cool thinking, so what if a Yank builds a crap house, and so what if it shakes and falls – no big deal! But I must admit, I was getting interested and Mr Williams was a great storyteller.

'Where did these fairies come from?' I asked.

'Some say they are descended from an ancient people who ruled Ireland long ago. When they were conquered by the Milesians, another ancient group, they went to live in caves around the Irish coast. Others say they are fallen angels who must do their Purgatory here on Earth; you can decide which to believe.'

When we said goodbye to Mr Williams, we promised to return the next day. He told us he would bring us to the well and to the place where the leprechaun was last seen.

'Won't that be dangerous?' asked Max.

'I think you will be safe enough,' smiled Mr Williams.

'I think the fairies have Max in a trance already,' laughed Joe.

When I reached home, our garden was full of dogs, ranging from small woolly balls of fluff to great hairy mutts. That would be bad enough only they had brought their five-year-old owners with them – the same lot who had taken over the garden the day before.

'What's going on?' I asked Mum.

'Oh! Stanley and Sylvester are having a doggie party for Ruff so he can meet some doggie pals.'

Sometimes I think Mum is a bit soft in the head.

'What a nice idea,' I pretended.

I climbed the stairs towards my bedroom, smiling. I needed peace and quiet to write down the information I had been given by Mr Williams.

INFORMATION AT LAST

On the following day Max, Joe and I were positively excited as we headed out the Ardsbeg Road. I had brought my camera as Roogie loves photographs.

Earlier I had taken Ruff for a walk but I had left him with the twins, as they had to go to a doggie party in one of their friend's gardens. Good, I thought, at least it would be some other poor sod and not me that would have to clean up doggie poo this evening!

Mr Williams was in his garden and he

waved to us when he saw us coming.

'As adults go, Mr Williams wasn't too bad,' I thought, as I waved back. He was easy to get to know and very friendly.

'Are you all ready for the big adventure?' he asked, as we came nearer. 'Just wait till I get my coat and then we'll go!'

The four of us then walked down the road to the old graveyard.

'It's through here,' said Mr Williams, 'but take care, as it's all overgrown. Very few people ever come here.'

Mr Williams beat away the brambles with a stick.

'Do you see a well over in that corner?' he asked.

Sure enough there was an old grey stone wall with steps leading down to a well.

'That well is hundreds of years old,' Mr Williams told us.

'Why would there be a well in a graveyard?' asked Max, which even for him was a clever enough question. After all, the dead would hardly need water?

'This well was a holy well, belonging to monks during the earlier centuries,' explained Mr Williams. 'We are now standing on the site of an ancient monastery. See, further up this field is a round stone ring. That is all that's left of the monks' round tower. I'm sure you have all learned about the round towers at school.'

'Weren't they the towers where the monks hid all their treasure when the Danes came?' asked Max. (Mr Roog would have been proud of him.)

'But what has all this to do with fairies and leprechauns?' I asked.

'Do you see that stone that Joe is sitting on?' asked Mr Williams. 'That is the exact spot where the leprechaun was seen.'

Joe jumped up in alarm.

'Does that mean that something terrible will happen to me?' he asked in fright.

'I doubt it,' laughed Mr Williams, but Joe didn't look too sure. He backed away from the stone as if it were a huge Alsatian, about to jump on him.

'Look!' Max winked at me. 'I think Joe is beginning to shrink.' We both started laughing.

'Leave Joe alone,' said Mr Williams. 'I don't know about you lot but I could do with something to eat. Why don't we go back to the house and I'll explain more to you about fairies there.'

'You lot go ahead,' I said, remembering my camera, 'I just want to take a few photos to prove to Roogie that we actually did do some research.'

However, as the footsteps of the others became more distant, I began to get just a little nervous.

'You can't let this get to you', I told myself.

As I stood there alone, looking around me, I imagined I could hear a swishing sound coming from under the hedgerow. It was time to get out of here, and as I chased down the road after the others I had the strangest feeling that little eyes were watching us – the eyes of the little folk!

Over the next few days we learned a lot about the 'wee folk'. They were said to hate a disbelieving person most of all. They could leave him/her with a stammer or cast a spell on his/her feet so that she couldn't stop dancing, or they could even put a hump on a disbeliever's back.

Secretly I was hoping that Mr Roog or Ben would find our research results hard to believe. I couldn't help but laugh as I imagined old Roogie dancing until he dropped or Ben developing a stammer until such time as he would go on his knees and beg for forgiveness. 'It would serve him right, the lousy git', was Joe's answer when I suggested it to him.

We learned that fairies were supposed to have the greatest power in November and also that in the same month, a red-haired man was supposed to have great power over the fairies. We took photographs of Mr Williams and his cottage.

Helen was delighted to pose for photographs too and insisted on changing into different outfits each time. When I asked Ben to pose, he gave me a look that let me know I was going a bit too far. Joe managed to smuggle an old photograph of him from the family album. In it, he had gaps in his teeth and his face was covered in pimples.

'It will serve him right if Mr Roog puts it on display in the school hall,' laughed Joe, and I couldn't agree more.

Talking of Helen and Ben – they were beginning to act very strangely as the Halloween holiday was coming to an end

and our project was taking shape. They took a very sudden interest in it. Ben was forever asking questions about Mr Williams, the graveyard and whether the leprechaun had actually been seen. Helen wanted to know what he looked like, was he big or small and what kind of clothes he was wearing when he appeared. They were always whispering to each other and were giggling a lot. If Joe, Max or I would come into the room the two of them would suddenly go silent. They were much nicer to us and Ben even allowed us into his room to see how the project was doing.

I didn't like it one bit but when I told Joe and Max, they shrugged their shoulders and said it was because the two of them were in love! I looked at them both – Joe with his spattering of freckles, ginger hair and toothy grin, Max who had mischief written all over him and whose nose permanently dripped snots. All of a sudden, they had become experts in the field of human emotions!

Then, I had to admit that they could be right – love did seem to make right sops of some people. Look at that silly Romeo and Juliet story that Miss Coll was always on about!

On Thursday evening Helen gave us three free tickets for the theatre where she worked. I began to feel guilty for thinking the worst of her.

'You will enjoy it,' she said, filing her long red nails. 'It is a very funny play – just what you three need before you go back to school on Monday. Ben and I are going out for a walk to see Mr Williams. We might take a few more photos. We should have the project finished by tomorrow.'

True to Helen's word the play was very funny. We rolled about in the seats laughing. We were in a good mood going home, knowing we could relax for the weekend. The project was almost finished. Old Roogie would be pleased. All was right with the world!

The Leprechaun of Lisnashee

I awoke next morning to the bleep of my mobile phone. It was Joe. He was so excited he could hardly speak.

'Holly! You just have to come over to my house right now. I think we have found a leprechaun.'

Before I was fully awake he was gone and when I tried to ring him back his phone was engaged. Silly little prat, I thought. I was just about to turn over in bed for a further snooze when my mum came into the room.

'Max and Helen are downstairs waiting for you,' she said, as she drew the curtain.

'They are wittering on about a leprechaun to your Dad. Really, that Helen Cooper should have more sense. I don't know what your Aunt Marjorie can be thinking of having that young lady visit Ben so often. Leprechauns indeed! Did you ever hear such nonsense?'

With that she left, muttering to herself. I could hear 'total waste of space' as she went back downstairs. I jumped out of bed, got washed quickly and ran down to the living room.

Max was gushing with excitement. 'Joe thinks he may have found a leprechaun,' he blurted out.

I blushed with embarrassment, as I knew my Dad could hear the conversation from his armchair.

'Oh! yeah,' said Dad. 'Definitely a leprechaun! The Snot Gang are becoming famous at last. Don't forget to bring him around to meet your mother and me. Make sure though that Ruff isn't in the garden when you bring him, as he might eat the poor little fellow up!' With that he leaned back in his chair and began to roar laughing. Tears rolled down his cheeks.

I was glad to feel the cold November air on my face as we shut the front door and followed Helen who tottered dangerously on her very high heels down the road in front of us. Joe met us at the door.

'Just wait until you see Ben's photographs,' he said, excitedly.

We went into the sitting room and Aunt Marjorie and Uncle Harry were examining a photograph under a magnifying glass.

'But it can't be!' Aunt Marjorie was saying. 'Everyone knows there are no such things as leprechauns, or are there? Now I don't know what to think. Look Holly!'

She was so excited she forgot to plant one of her usual smackers on my face. I could hardly believe what I was looking at. There, in the photograph, was a little man standing in the graveyard near the well.

He had a long beard and was dressed in a grey and brown tweed coat. I thought that Max's two eyes were going to pop out of his head.

'What a cute little man,' said Helen. 'Couldn't you just hug him?'

'I see nothing cute about the little twirp,' glowered Ben, who is a very jealous type. 'He definitely wasn't there yesterday. Ask Mr Williams.'

Just then the doorbell rang.

58

'That will be Mr Williams now,' said Uncle Harry, as he went to open the floor.

When Mr Williams looked at the photograph he agreed with Ben.

'There was no one to be seen in that graveyard when that photo was taken. I think we may be on to something here.'

'Yippee!' shouted Joe, as he and Max slapped their hands off one another as boys do to prove how silly they really are.

'Roogie will never believe us when we go back to school,' said Max. 'He will think it's another one of our tricks.'

'You could hardly blame him,' answered Helen. 'When I think of all the tricks that you three played on that poor man.'

'Yeah! Like the time you hid his glasses,' interrupted Ben.

'Then there was that time that Joe and Holly sent a Valentine card to Miss Coll from Mr Roog.'

'Seems like you three have quite a reputation for playing tricks on people,' laughed Mr Williams.

'You haven't heard the half of it. There is hardly a person left in Lisnashee that those three haven't played a joke on,' added Uncle Harry.

Up until now Mr Williams thought we were three model, hard-working kids! I felt ashamed of my past and could feel my face getting red.

'Now we have to find a way to make this leprechaun show himself,' said Mr Williams, still looking at the photograph.

'Gosh! Do you think you could do that?' asked Joe, looking at Mr Williams as if he was a genius, whilst Aunt Marjorie went out to the kitchen to make everyone a cup of tea.

'According to my book,' said Mr Williams, 'if you can locate a leprechaun and have a sighting of him, as we have in this photograph, it is easy to get him to reveal himself.'

'Gosh! You are so clever, Mr Williams,' answered Helen, looking at him with admiration. 'How do we go about it?'

'Well, it says in my book that a person with ginger hair has great power over the leprechauns in the month of November,' said Mr Williams.

'Oh no, you don't,' said Joe, as he realised everyone was looking in his direction. 'I saw in a book where the fairy folk can turn a person into a rat or a frog or something nasty.'

'Whatever it is, it's got to be an improvement on what is already there,' laughed Ben. 'Are you going to help us or not?'

'Alright, I suppose I will,' replied Joe, not looking too sure of himself.

'Good! That is settled,' said Mr Williams. 'After we drink this tea we will head out to the graveyard to see what we can find.'

'You had better wear more suitable shoes Helen,' said Aunt Marjorie, as she ran to the press under the stairs and fished out a pair of large garden wellies.

'Bu ... bu ... but these shoes are perfectly comfy,' stammered Helen, looking with total horror at the geeky wellies. Max and I had to hide behind Uncle Harry to keep us from bursting out laughing.

'Nonsense!' barged Aunt Marjorie. 'How could you walk through a graveyard wearing those!' She pointed with contempt at Helen's delicate high heels. Everyone looked down. Helen's perfectly polished toenails winked out from behind bright red peep toe shoes. She looked to Ben for help.

'I know,' Ben said. 'We can go by Helen's house and she can get another outfit there.' At this stage we were almost smothered laughing and I could see a definite twinkle in Mr Williams' eyes as well.

As we walked down the path behind Helen's tottering heels, Uncle Harry shouted, 'Don't forget to bring me back a pot of gold'.

'Some people haven't the sense they were born with,' muttered Aunt Marjorie, as she closed the door.

'That was a close shave,' sighed Helen with relief. 'I was sure I would have to wear those ghastly green wellies.'

When we reached Helen's house it was obvious the news had arrived before us. Aunt Marjorie had been on the phone. I was surprised that Mr and Mrs Cooper seemed to be so interested in our story.

We had to go through the whole story again and show them the photograph. They appeared to be genuinely interested. I couldn't understand it at all. When I whispered this to Ben he said it was because they had great respect for Mr Williams and not because they would believe little twirps like us!

On our way out to the graveyard Mr Williams explained to us that Joe would be the only one who could go into the graveyard.

'The rest of us will have to keep out of sight,' he warned. 'Joe will have to command the leprechaun in a very firm voice to show himself.'

'What if the leprechaun doesn't want to come out?' asked Joe, looking frightened.

'That will depend on the tone of voice you use,' laughed Mr Williams. 'You will have to say it very slowly and be very firm when you give the command.' I began to envy Joe his mop of bright ginger hair.

Meanwhile, Ben and Helen were walking some distance behind and giggling and whispering, as usual. Ben scowled when I dropped back to join them. I whispered to them, 'You don't suppose that Mr Williams may have gone a bit funny in the head, do you? I mean let's face it. The chances of a leprechaun being in that graveyard are very small.'

'Then how can you explain the photo-graph?' asked Helen. 'Of course there is a leprechaun. Just you wait and see.'

At this stage I was beginning to despair of the whole lot of them. Max and Joe I could explain. They still believed in the tooth fairy. Helen too I could understand. She wasn't exactly the brightest star in the sky. But Mr Williams? Mr and Mrs Cooper? Aunt Marjorie and Uncle Harry?

And now Ben? This was the cousin that I had always secretly looked up to, despite his bad manners!

Had the whole world lost the plot or was I the only one, to quote Aunt Marjorie, that still had the sense I was born with?

Titch O'Flynn

It was late afternoon by the time we got to the graveyard. The sky in the distance was a strange mixture of greys, purples and reds. The little bent trees looked ghostly in the lonely graveyard. Joe was not too happy.

'Now remember,' advised Mr Williams, 'don't show any fear. Your command must be very clear. Say very slowly – leprechaun! I know you are here! Show yourself!'

'But what if the leprechaun appears and takes me away with him to the fairy world?'

stammered Joe, almost ready to cry.

'No such luck!' I thought to myself.

'I'm sorry, I can't go in there alone,' Joe continued.

Max pulled him aside and whispered, 'Listen Joe! Do you want Ben to find out all about that photograph of him that you intend showing all around the school?' That convinced him.

'You must all come running if you hear me shouting,' Joe said.

'Good man yourself!' Mr Williams said with delight, clapping him on the back. 'Don't worry, we will be hiding behind these trees just outside the graveyard wall.'

'You are so brave,' gushed Helen, as she landed a big kiss right on Joe's cheek.

'Aw! Yuck! Why did you have to go and do that? That is disgusting!'

'Oh! Go on in,' said Ben crossly, 'and don't be such a coward.'

We all watched while Joe slowly made his way through the brambles to the area beside the wall. He looked scared. He shouted out in a nervous tone as Mr Williams had told him.

'Leprechaun! I know you are there! Come out now!'

For a few seconds nothing happened and then, from behind the walls of the old ruined monastery a small, plumpish man stepped out. Joe nearly did a runner. I expected him to be dressed all in green but this little man was dressed in brown, just as in the photograph Ben had taken. A long white beard reached his toes.

Joe's two eyes were like saucers as he backed away. Suddenly his courage came back.

'I command you not to move from that spot,' said Joe. However, he soon backed off when the little man stamped his foot in anger.

'Bad cess to ya! Let me go!' At this stage we thought we had better go to Joe's rescue. We ran into the graveyard.

'That you may all die roaring like Doran's ass,' shouted the wee man.

Before I could ask politely who Doran

was the little man got redder and redder with anger, as he shook his fists at us.

'That you may all screech with awful thirst and may your brains and eyeballs burst!'

'What a charming little man,' laughed Mr Williams.

Ben, meanwhile, was busy taking footage with his camcorder.

'Keep your hair on!' said Max crossly. 'No one is going to harm you.'

Helen was giggling to herself, as usual, while Joe looked dumbstruck, as if he had seen a ghost.

'Bad cess to all of you,' shouted the leprechaun again. 'Don't think that you will get your hands on my gold, because you won't, so there!' and again he stamped his foot in anger.

My temper got the better of me at this stage. 'Listen, you little ill-mannered creep – we don't want your gold.'

Meanwhile, Joe and Max were walking around the little man looking at his heavy brogue shoes with two large buckles, and his tweed hat.

'Sod off!' he shouted at them.

'Gosh!' said Max. 'You have loads of wrinkles'.

'Faith, then! You are no oil paintin' yourself,' said the leprechaun. Everyone laughed.

'Listen!' said Mr Williams. 'Max is right. No one is going to harm you. Now, tell us about yourself.'

'I will and my eyeball,' shouted the leprechaun. 'Don't be so nosy! I'm telling you nuthin'.'

Mr Williams called over to Joe, 'Command him to tell us.'

Joe looked crossly at the little man. 'I command you to answer every question you are asked.' We thought we could hear the leprechaun saying something like 'bossy wee runt' but we couldn't be certain.

'I can't promise it will be all the truth you will hear from Titch O'Flynn,' he replied cheekily. 'What do you want to know so that I can get away?'

'Are there any other leprechauns around?' I asked him.

'They are scattered here and there over the bogs and hills of Ireland, from Donegal to Cork and from Galway to Dublin,' the little man replied.

'How come we can't see them then?' asked Joe.

'You wouldn't see me either if you had-n't tricked me!' answered Titch O'Flynn. 'Now, little red-haired man! Let me go this instant or the curse of Titch O Flynn will fall on you.' At this, poor Joe looked very frightened. Titch saw his chance.

'Be the hokey! Is that a crowd of lep-rechauns that I am after seein', comin' in that gate over there?' he said, as he point-ed his finger in the direction of the gate.

We all turned to look and when we looked back again Titch O'Flynn was run-ning away in the distance through the long grass and brambles, until he disappeared behind a wall.

'Let's follow him!' shouted Joe.

'It is too late,' replied Mr Williams. 'You have no more power over him. Let him go. We have seen and heard enough. Anyway, we have it all on film.'

'Just wait until the people of Lisnashee hear this story,' said Max. 'We will be famous'.

'Yes,' I replied. 'People from all over the world will get to hear about us. We might even be on telly!'

Max was off on cloud nine as I was speaking. He was imagining it all before his eyes. I looked at Joe and Joe looked at me. It was easy to see that Max was a brother of Helen's. They both shared the same brain cell!

Mr Williams laughed. 'Certainly things will not be as dull for you all in the next few weeks!'

It was getting dark when we reached the town. As I saw the lights of Lisnashee in the distance I wondered was our town ready for our big discovery? How would the people react to the news that they had a real, live leprechaun living among them? We could hardly wait to find out!

THE NEWS GETS OUT

My Dad was the first to hear the news.

'Titch O'Flynn,' he laughed. 'You kids are wasted in a small town like Lisnashee. With your imagination you should be writing scripts for movies.' He called Mum.

'Did you hear that, Sue? Our daughter, Holly, has discovered a real life leprechaun living out in some old graveyard. We will be famous. I won't ever need to go to work again.'

I could feel my face go red with embarrassment.

'I know it sounds corny,' I said, 'but we really did see a leprechaun and if you don't believe us you can go and ask Mr Williams.'

'What has Mr Williams to do with it?' enquired Mum, as she came on from the kitchen wiping her fingers on a towel. At least she has the grace not to laugh I thought.

Max and Joe then joined in and told the whole story from beginning to end. There could be little doubt these two boys had seen something, such was the enthusiasm with which each described the leprechaun and all they had seen. Looking at my Mum and Dad's faces it seemed as if they were beginning to believe at least part of our story.

'You know you will all be the laughing stock of the town if you are making any of this up,' warned Dad. 'Sue,' he said to my Mum. 'You had better get Joe and Max's parents over to see what they think of it all. I will ring Mr Williams.'

'That is a good idea,' agreed Mum. 'Now children, you go into the kitchen and get something to eat. I'll ring Mr and Mrs

Cooper, and ask Uncle Harry and Aunt Marjorie to come around. Oh dear! Why you all have to go pottering around in old graveyards I'll never know. I'm quite sure someone is playing a trick on you all.'

Then she went out into the kitchen. Dad went off to ring Mr Williams. When he came back he told us that Mr Williams was on the way. He had something important to tell us all. Ten minutes later the doorbell rang.

'This better be worth hearing,' said Aunt Marjorie, in a threatening way, as she arrived at the door. 'I'm sure people don't feel like leaving their warm homes on a cold November night to listen to some tall story or other about leprechauns.'

'I agree with you dear,' said Uncle Harry, following meekly behind.

'Why does he always agree?' I asked myself. 'Why couldn't he disagree just for once?'

Mr and Mrs Cooper were next to arrive, followed by Mr Williams with Ben and Helen in tow. Aunt Marjorie was the first to speak.

'I'm very surprised at you, Mr Williams, that a man of your standing in the community could believe such nonsense?'

Please don't let Uncle Harry say 'I agree dear', I thought, and for the first time ever he didn't.

However, there was a surprise to follow. Mr Williams looked at my Dad and said, 'Will you explain or will I Seán?'

I looked over at my Dad and saw a very definite twinkle in his eye.

'Actually, I have a confession to make to you all,' he continued, and he was hardly able to control his laughter. 'When I first heard of this project I thought, why not play a Halloween trick on Holly and the boys. After all, they have spent their short lives up until now playing tricks on everyone else.'

Max, Joe and I looked at him in disbelief.

'I got the help of Helen and Ben,' he continued. 'I heard the children had gone to visit Mr Williams so I organised his help too.'

I looked at Mr Williams in horror. He had betrayed us, but how? We did see a leprechaun and he spoke to us. How could that be?

'As you know,' my Dad went on, 'Helen works at the theatre. One of the actors agreed to take the part of the leprechaun. The theatre had lots of costumes so there was no problem getting him dressed.'

We looked in disgust at Helen who had the grace to look sheepish.

'You mean there never was a leprechaun,' wailed Joe, as the truth sank in.

It takes Joe a while to cop on to what people are saying.

'Of all the mean, dirty, rotten tricks,' shouted Max.

'This is priceless,' laughed Aunt Marjorie. 'To think I was complaining about leaving my warm house tonight! I wouldn't miss this for the world and the best part is that the trick is on the three of *them* for a change. Oh dear!' And she rubbed her eyes with a handkerchief.

Aunt Marjorie is a bit like a bowlful of jelly. When she laughs, all her parts wobble.

Mum was the only one who felt sorry for us.

'Oh Seán! How mean can you get?'

'Just payback time. Gotcha!' laughed my Dad. 'Do you remember the time those three found all your old love letters tied up with blue ribbon in the attic and went around the town playing postman. Oh yes! I have a very good memory.'

'They were only five or six years old at the time,' Mum added, defending us, but getting red as she remembered.

'Then there was the time they decided to paint our garden shed in bright pink,' remembered Dad. As he spoke he was giving the others ideas.

'Yeah!' said Ben, seething with anger as he spoke. 'There was that time they sent my photo and a letter to that geeky O'Grady girl asking for a date.'

'Now you mention it,' remarked Helen, looking as if she got a brainwave. 'I never did find out who sent me that typed letter from a model agency, telling me they saw my photo in the paper at the graduation dance and they wanted to offer me a modelling contract. I went around for weeks walking on air only to find out the whole thing was a hoax.' She was almost ready to cry with the memory.

Now it was our turn to look sheepish. Even Uncle Harry was beginning to warm up!

'There was that time the radio station rang me up to ask about my prize begonias.'

My poor mother was looking in horror at

the three of us. Mr Williams looked as if he was really enjoying himself.

'Sorry kids!' he said cheerfully. 'When your Dad told me about the way you have been playing tricks on people all these years I was only too glad to help him get his own back.'

I looked around in dismay at all these adults. For years we had trusted them, depended on them, and now this! I was speechless. Max and Joe were threatening Helen and Ben already.

'You two just wait,' they said. 'You just wait.'

THE SILLY BILLIES

I suppose we should be thankful, I thought to myself. At least only the close family members know. They can hardly afford to laugh at anyone. Imagine how ashamed we would be if the rest of the people of Lisnashee found out. As Joe, Max and I sat in my bedroom on that Saturday afternoon before going back to school we consoled ourselves with that thought.

However, we didn't know that Ben and Helen were out to get 'blood' and that they had enlisted the help of Stanley and

Sylvester, with their 'doggie pals'.

'Your sister is very silly,' explained Ben, patiently, as he sat the two of them down with two packets of Smarties. 'She told everyone that she saw a little fairy man. Joe and Max thought they saw him too. They told everyone. But it was only a trick! They are not very clever. Now everyone is laughing at them. A good name for them would be "the three silly Billies!"'

Stanley and Sylvester were delighted, as name calling was their strong point. They would make certain that word got around. When Max, Joe and I went over to Mrs Muldoon's sweet shop that evening the name Silly Billies rang out from over the walls of different gardens. It was so embarrassing. It was bad enough being called 'The Snot Gang' without getting another title. Worse was to follow.

'Ah! The three detectives!' smiled Mrs Muldoon, as the little bell on her shop door tinkled. 'I heard that you found your leprechaun.'

This was in front of two other customers!

We bought three chocolate bars quickly and left the shop, our faces red.

'There should be a law against this sort of thing,' grumbled Joe. 'How will we face going back to school?'

'You have just given me an idea,' I said. 'There is a law. People are not allowed to tease people in public. We will go straight down and make a complaint. I just know Ben and Helen are behind this. Come on!'

When we reached the police station, Tom and his friend were behind the desk having a cup of coffee.

'Well, well! If it isn't "The Snot Gang",' said Tom's friend.

'I wouldn't use that word "well" if I were you,' answered Tom. 'That could be a sore point.' With that the two of them spluttered laughing. They were a sorry pair! I decided to ignore them.

'We have come to make a complaint!' I declared, and Joe and Max nodded.

'Hold on until I get my notebook,' said

Tom's friend. At last I felt we were being taken seriously.

'Now,' said the policeman, opening a large book. 'Do you want to complain that Titch O'Flynn was impersonating a leprechaun or that a leprechaun was impersonating Titch O'Flynn. Which one?'

We stood looking at him with our mouths open. We were ruined. Even the very small details of the story had leaked out. Who else knew? How would we live it down?

A hundred questions ran through our brains as we stood looking at the two smirking caps behind the desk.

As if they knew what we were thinking, the one called Tom said, 'If you like, we could give you all a new identity, change your looks, hair colour, etc., and arrange for you all to be sent to an unknown address. We could even arrange to send you out of the country.'

It only took those few pathetic words to make the one not called Tom to double up and say 'Stop! Tom! You are killing me!' as large tears of laughter rolled down his face.

Max, Joe and I left the station. We had never felt so down in our lives.

That was bad enough but worse was to follow. When we arrived at Aunt Marjorie's, who was visiting but Uncle Frank and Aunt Amy?

'Found your leprechaun then?' enquired Uncle Frank. 'You must bring him over to meet us. I'm sure he is an expert on bog oak. I could do with his advice'. Then he laughed, as if the whole thing was very amusing.

'Now dear!' said Aunt Amy. 'It is not right to tease them. They are only children. I'm sure there are lots of things they could tease you about too, if they wanted.' 'You could say that again!' I thought, but at least I was grateful to her because apart from my Mum, she was the only person who had shown us any sympathy until now.

That Sunday was the shortest Sunday of my entire life. I was looking at the clock, willing the minute hand to go much slower. I didn't want to face school on Monday.

Did you ever notice though that when you want a day to go slowly it goes very fast? All too soon it was Monday morning and we had to face back to school.

CONGRATULATIONS!

Well, at least we had our project finished. We decided to include the pictures and film of Titch O'Flynn, to show what a leprechaun might look like. We had plenty of photographs and drawings, a map of the old graveyard, some very good research material on the fairy folk, and overall a well-presented project.

As we had guessed we got plenty of teasing in the school yard and one or two of the teachers had a laugh at our expense.

Mr Roog was busy sorting out all the

entries for judging. A big poster on the notice board read that the entries would be judged by a person from the Tourist Board.

Wednesday was the day when the winners would be announced. That day, a message came to our classroom to say that Joe, Max and I were wanted in the Principal's office immediately.

Max knocked on the door nervously, as most of his visits to the office in the past hadn't been pleasant ones! When we walked in we found the Principal, Mr Roog and a man who introduced himself as Paul from the Tourist Board.

'Congratulations,' he said, as he smiled and shook our hands. 'Your project is superb. It has given us lots of ideas. You have drawn our attention to the old graveyard and monastery at Ardsbeg and you have done some excellent research on the fairy folk. I want to congratulate all three of you and your teacher Mr Roog for this wonderful project.'

'A fat lot he had to do with it,' I thought, as I smiled sweetly at the man.

'Your school will be given a brand new computer and each of you will be given a new laptop to help you to do future research,' he added.

'Yipee!' shouted Max and Joe together, as they forgot where they were and clapped their hands up against each other in the silly way that boys do. Somehow, I couldn't imagine the two of them doing much more research!

'We are all very proud of you,' smiled the Principal. 'You are a credit to the school.'

'I agree with that,' smiled Mr Roog, his gold tooth glinting in the sun. 'Congratulations!'

That afternoon the results were announced and the photographer from the local paper came in to take our photographs. We could hardly wait until Friday, when the paper was published. We ran to Mrs Muldoon's shop just as she opened.

There on the front page was a picture of Max, Joe and I. The caption read 'S'NOT WHAT IT SEEMS! Then underneath we read, *The Snot Gang Discover History in Lisnashee*. We bought two copies and ran to the police station with one of them, where we left it on the desk.

'The laugh is on them now,' said Joe, as he spread the other paper out on his sitting-room table.

When he read the article, Ben was

disgusted. 'I wouldn't mind but those three dorks did nothing. It was Helen and I who did all the work!'

'Oh, leave them alone Ben!' said Aunt Marjorie. 'Let them enjoy their little moment of fame.'

'That's right!' said Max. 'Talk about us as if we are not here. We don't mind.'

Uncle Harry laughed. 'I think it is a good project. Look at this notice!'

We all looked and read:

Notice from the Tourist Board.

A public meeting will be held in Lisnashee Town Hall at 8pm on Monday to discuss the development of the old monastery, fairy fort and graveyard at Ardsbeg as a possible tourist attraction.

'Imagine it was all our idea,' remarked Joe, forgetting it was really my idea!

Our fame spread quickly. Everywhere we went people were coming up to us and saying 'Well done!' For years Lisnashee had just been sitting on a map. Nothing ever happened here. Nothing changed. Few people from outside the town ever came to visit. Now the adults were talking about how that might change.

'It will be good for the town,' said Aunt Amy.

'It is about time someone did something,' muttered Uncle Frank. Uncle Frank always has to grumble! Of course, it never occurs to him to 'do something' himself.

A New Leisure Centre

That Monday night Joe, Max and I set out for the Town Hall. The place was already packed when we arrived. Almost everyone in Lisnahee was there, including Mr Williams, who was chairing the meeting. He stood up and introduced our man from the Tourist Board. He was interested in our project and wanted ideas on how best to use the information in our project to attract tourists to Lisnashee.

'There is a lot of history in this area,' Mr Williams began. 'We have the ruins of an old monastery and graveyard at Ardsbeg and we also have a town named after the fairy folk. We invite you now to put forward any ideas you may have.'

The first to stand up was Mr Roog.

'I think this town needs a museum,' he said, 'and an historical centre to inculcate a sense of heritage and culture in the people.'

'What is that old bat on about now?' whispered Max in my ear. 'What does inculcate mean?'

'Oh, never mind,' I whispered.

'Silly git!' whispered Helen on the other side. 'Who needs an old boring museum?'

Then, before anyone could stop her, and smiling sweetly, she stood up.

'No, chairperson! I think a health and beauty farm would help the town more.'

The Tourist Board man had just lifted a glass of water to take a sip and he almost choked. I could see the faint sign of a smile on Mr Williams' face.

There was silence. God knows I had to agree with Helen that we needed a health and beauty farm when I looked around that room and saw the mixture of bald domes, fat bellies and a general mix of very unhealthy looking humans.

'Did no one think of a park?' stammered my Uncle Harry meekly. The poor man had been so ground down by Aunt Marjorie for years, he even surprised himself. Up stood Aunt Marjorie and ignored the chairperson. She spoke to Uncle Harry.

'Harold dear! No one is interested in your potted plants and flowers. Make a sensible suggestion if you are making one!' I felt so sorry for Uncle Harry, as his face went red.

'Perhaps Holly, Max or Joe might like to say something? After all, it is because of their project that we are here,' suggested Mr Williams.

I was very tempted to suggest a training centre for adults where they could be programmed to understand children better, but instead I asked could we have a few minutes to confer with one another.

Finally, Max stood up to deliver our idea.

'We think the children and young people in this town have very little to do or have few places to go. We would like to see a swimming pool and leisure centre in the town – also, a playground for children'.

At this point the man from the Tourist Board stood up and said, 'Your idea would certainly be good for tourism and for the area. I think we could look into that.' Everyone looked impressed.

'I have some land out the Ardsbeg Road that is of no use to me. I am going to donate that to the town,' declared Mr Williams. Everyone gasped. Then, there was loud clapping.

'As it is near the old monastery and graveyard, it would provide a good site for some of the suggestions made this evening. We will then have to set up a committee to look into all the ideas put before us. I myself would like to see a heritage centre and in this centre we could put Mr Roog's museum.'

I looked over at Mr Roog. He looked like a cat who had just got a bowl of cream!

'Beside the heritage centre we could build a sports and leisure centre.' It was our turn to look pleased. Then looking at Helen, Mr Williams continued, 'Perhaps we could even manage to put a health and beauty room in it!' Now Helen looked pleased.

'Lastly I would suggest that these buildings should be surrounded by a public park and play area for the children. Mr

Harry Cooper might like to help us to plan that one, as he knows a lot about gardening and such matters.' I stole a look at Uncle Harry. He looked ready to explode with happiness.

'Good old Mr Williams,' I thought, even though I was still mad at him for playing the trick on us. I had to admit, he had a way of making people feel good about themselves.

'We will meet again in a week's time to form a committee,' he continued. Then he thanked everyone for coming, invited them to put any further suggestions into a 'suggestion box' that would be in Mrs Muldoon's shop, and asked them to have a cup of tea.

A committee was set up the following week and Mr Williams' ideas were accepted, as well as a few others from the locality. The committee was very impressed with the photograph of Titch O'Flynn and because the picture was a great likeness of what a leprechaun would actually look like, it was blown up into a huge picture for the front of the centre. It will be unveiled when the centre is opened next year and the name of the centre will be the 'Titch O'Flynn Heritage and Leisure Centre'.

Uncle Frank has offered to do a large oak sculpture of Titch O'Flynn for the front entrance and work has already started on the building itself.

Now Max, Joe and I are back into our usual routine. Helen is still seeing Ben at weekends. I can't imagine what those two have in common but Max, Joe and I agree they deserve each other!

People still tease us about the trick that was played on us in the graveyard. However, we are 'big' enough to let them think they are having the last laugh!

Our minds are actively looking for new victims to work on. The Snot Gang haven't gone away! We have designs on the two policemen even as I speak!

Meanwhile, we are looking forward to the new leisure centre and swimming pool. Life in Lisnashee will never be the same again!